The Leprechaun Under the Bed

by **TERESA BATEMAN**

illustrated by

PAUL MEISEL

Holiday House / New York

For Eva and Kaden—
may you grow to appreciate
the value of a good friend.
And for Scotty—welcome!
T. B.

For "Cam" Campbell Clark
(the person responsible
for my children being ¼ Irish!)
Love,
P. M.

Text copyright © 2012 by Teresa Bateman

Illustrations copyright © 2012 by Paul Meisel

All Rights Reserved

HOLIDAY HOUSE is registered in the U.S. Patent and Trademark Office.

Printed and Bound in November 2011 at Tien Wah Press,

Johor Bahru, Johor, Malaysia.

The text typeface is Gryphius.

The illustrations were done with acrylic and watercolor paints

on Arches watercolor paper.

www.holidayhouse.com

First Edition

1 3 5 7 9 10 8 6 4 2

Library of Congress Cataloging-in-Publication Data

Bateman, Teresa.

The leprechaun under the bed / by Teresa Bateman ; illustrated by Paul Meisel. — 1st ed.

p. cm.

Summary: Brian the leprechaun enjoys his solitary life until

a human builds a stone cottage above Brian's underground home.

ISBN 978-0-8234-2221-0 (hardcover)

[1. Leprechauns—Fiction. 2. Friendship—Fiction.]

I. Meisel, Paul, ill. II. Title.

PZ7.B294435Le 2012

[E]—dc22

2011007364

B RIAN O'S H E A enjoyed his privacy.
"A leprechaun can be alone without being lonely,"
he liked to say. Indeed, he would know, for he made a snug
home beneath the ground in an out-of-the-way spot.

But time went on. Big tall human people moved nearer and nearer, until one day a man named Sean MacDonald started building a stone cottage right overhead.

Brian tried leprechaun magic to stop Sean. He made Sean see headless ghosts and even a banshee rising from the foundation stones of his new cottage.

But his plan backfired.

"It's just like my sainted mother always told me," Sean declared in delight. "The land of Ireland is full of magic and surprises!"

All too soon a fine cottage stood over Brian's home, so he built a door under Sean's bed.

On moonlit nights Brian would cobble outside. When it rained, he worked under Sean's bed, deliberately disturbing the man's sleep.

Yet he didn't wish to be discovered, so, if Sean moved, Brian would whisper, "Now don't you be fretting your wee little head. It's only the cat under the bed."

After a week of restless nights Sean decided he had to know why he wasn't sleeping well. He went to bed as usual; but, though his eyes were closed, his ears were open.

At midnight the tapping began, and Sean sat bolt upright.

"Now don't you be fretting your wee little head. It's only the cat under the bed," he heard from below.

"Ah, of course . . . the cat . . ." Sean yawned, settling back under the covers. Then his eyes flew open. "I don't have a cat!" he thought. "And even if I did, whoever heard of a talking cat?"

TAP
TAP
TAP

TAP
TAP
TAP

So, what was under the bed? The answer popped into his head.

Sean smiled. His mother had always said that a leprechaun in the house was a fine piece of luck. Luck he couldn't afford to lose.

The next morning Sean made stirabout for breakfast and placed a bowl of it under the bed for the "cat."

At lunch the bowl was empty, so he put in some stew. From that day on, every time he filled his own plate he added a bit to the bowl under the bed.

Sean was a hardworking man, but his small farm produced barely enough. Times grew hard and times grew harder until there came a day when Sean went to bed with both his stomach and the bowl empty.

The next morning a gold coin gleamed in the middle of the kitchen table.

"What a blessing it is to have a cat in the house," he remarked aloud before hurrying out to buy good food.

They lived well for weeks on that coin; but soon the cupboard was bare again, and another gold coin appeared.

"Consider this a loan," Sean said, "until times are better. Thank you, 'Cat.'"

But when Sean went to buy his oatmeal and potatoes, there was more than one eyebrow raised in the village.

A poor man might have saved one gold coin for hard times, but two?

Gossip ran like water through fingers, and as it spread it grew: Sean MacDonald must have a whole chest of gold coins hidden in his cottage!

What many tongues say, be it true or not, many ears
hear. Two robbers caught wind of the tale and decided that
no one deserved Sean's gossiped gold more than they did.
One crisp, dry morning they hid outside, waiting for
Sean to leave. Then they slipped into his cottage,
tossed the cupboards, and pried stones
out of the fireplace.

Such a clatter made Brian poke his head up
from under the bed. He was shocked at what he saw,
but what happened next was worse. The cottage door
swung open as Sean returned for a forgotten tool.

In no more time than it takes to tell, the robbers tied the poor man to a chair.

"Tell us where you've hidden the gold," they bellowed.

Fearing for Sean's safety, Brian banged his hammer against the floor to catch the robbers' attention.

"Eh now, what's that?" one of the men asked.

Fearing for Brian's safety, Sean spoke quickly. "Now don't you be fretting your wee little head. It's only the cat under the bed."

"Cat?" the man replied. "Well, the bed's the only place we haven't looked." As Sean worried, Brian grinned. Both robbers stuck their heads under the bed, and there they saw exactly what Brian had told them: a cat.

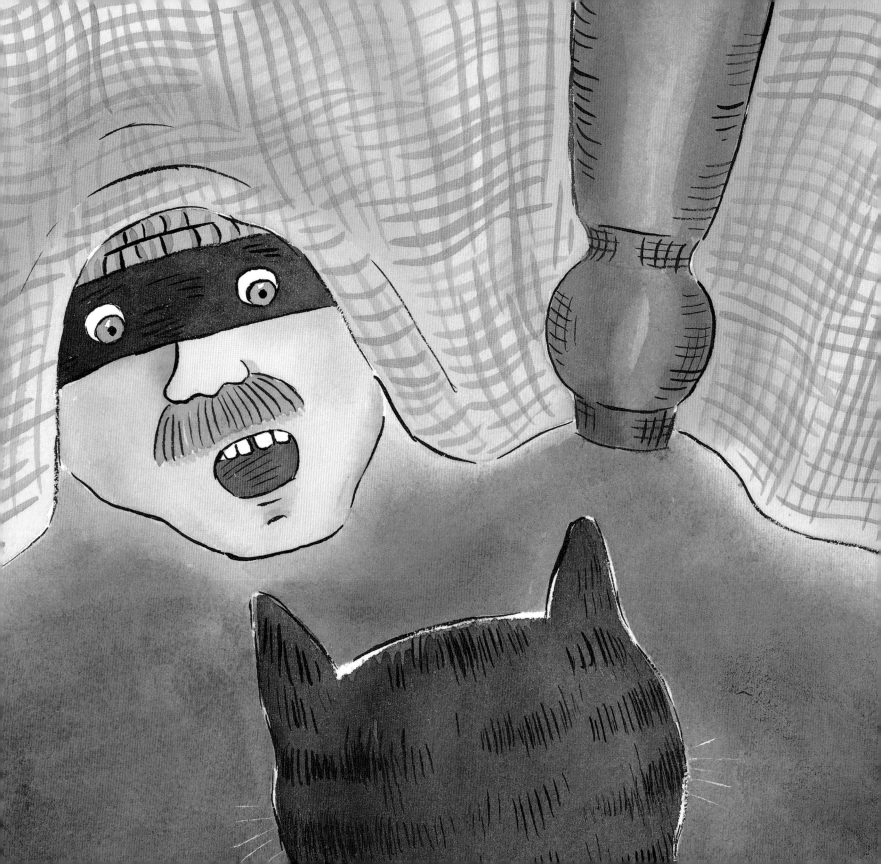

But this was a wildcat: eyes like lightning and claws like knives. The cat smiled at the robbers, then licked its lips as if it found the sight of them . . . tasty.

With a shriek, the men tumbled backward, then fled
as if the devil himself were at their heels.

Brian
laughed till
tears ran down
his cheeks.

Sean chuckled as well as he wiggled free of the rope. Then he stretched, and bowed in the direction of his pillow.

"'Tis a grand thing, indeed, having a 'cat' beneath the bed," he declared.

"Aye," replied a voice from below, "and it's a pleasure having a friend above it."

And they lived well
and happily for the rest
of their days.